ME and Him

ME and Him

David Dayan Fisher

ME and Him

Published by Sunnyfields Publishing

The right of David Dayan Fisher to be identified as the Author of the Work has been asserted by him in accordance with the Copyright, Designs and Patents Act 1988.

All rights reserved. No part of this publication may be reproduced in a retrieval system or transmitted by any means, electronic or mechanical, photocopying or otherwise, without the prior permission of the copyright holders.

Written by David Dayan Fisher

Cover Design by Patricia Krebs
Book Design by *wordzworth.com*

ISBN: 978-1-4993-0132-8

About the Author

David Dayan Fisher is a consummate artist, a renaissance man. Primarily an actor with a full resume in Hollywood movies and TV shows, he is also an author, an artist of abstract art, and a poet of adult and children's poems. He never wanted to stop playing as a child, and seems to have created the perfect life doing so.

This is David's eighth book. He is inspired by normal human beings, called spiritual leaders and prophets, from thousands of years ago to the present day, and includes these messages within the text of his writings.

This is a story, told by a little boy and based on truth, about the untruths that cover our real connection and joy in life.

Him is not fictional.

We are all incredibly special beings who have been made to feel rather not so.

Hopefully this wonderful story will bring some light into the cloudy days of life.

CHAPTER ONE

It makes me very happy to know that someone else is going to read my story. I'm me. My name is not important. In fact, most of what I will tell you about me isn't really that important. It's all just a story of the clothes put on me by others. What is important is how I learned about that very fact. Once, I was so lost in my clothes; I had totally forgotten about the real truth of me, the truth of all of us, before we were dressed by others.

Anyway, let's get back to the story of me. Me, before I met Him. I was born. From that very moment, others started to dress me. I was given a hat, as a name. I soon had some trousers in the form of a family background, with a history, which gave me a shirt, in the shape of a religion, and then some socks and underpants of values, which ranged from class, diet, hates, and political views. Oh, and now and then, depending on the seasons, I got to wear a tie, in the form of a side to support in a football team. This clothing that was put on me seemed to fit for a while. From the true me, I became the me of others. I was clothed by my family and everyone around us. But, in time, I started to see how my clothes would keep me away from others and make others see me differently and even dislike me. I saw how everyone was labeled and made to seem better or less because of what they were clothed in. I couldn't understand this odd, broken life and knew somehow, deep down, we were all the same, all equal, no matter who wore what clothes.

I came from a normal background. Middle class, I was told. I had a mum and a dad and two brothers, who were both older than me. But most important to me was my dog, Sunny.

For a while I fit my clothes, but soon my home life started to fall apart. My mum and my dad became different to each other and everything got more angry and unhappy. The fun faded and the memories of it did also. What was left of the good was now virtually all gone. Everything was wrong. My brothers and I became problems to our whole family, and we were used in arguments. Home did not feel like home anymore. It was more like a battlefield. But I always had Sunny to go to, to find shelter from the bombs and bullets of the war. Eventually, as I remember, my dad was never there. In fact, it seems he never was. My clothes got more uncomfortable as I started to grow out of them, and my life became more upsetting to the point that, if I did not have Sunny, I started to have thoughts of somehow either running away or ending the pain.

School was for me, unlike most, a great escape from home. But still there were so many others running around trying to make their clothes fit or find new ones that others would like. They all seemed somewhat happy with the way life had dressed them. I was good at sports and less than good with school work. It seemed to be all confused and mixed up with my tight clothes, but I was not stupid. An average student, so I kept hearing. "He could do better" was the tune that followed me. I had good friends who wore different clothes than me, but we all liked each other for how we felt without those things put on us. When we were alone, we could see each other for our true selves. We could throw off the lies. We spent our times dreaming of new ways to be dressed, new lives we could lead. We became rebels to those who had nicely dressed lives.

The teachers told me I needed to tidy myself up, which made my mother also say the same thing. Somehow, something did not fit. I was growing out of my clothes but had no choice but to wear them. I had a war at home, no real care for school work, and I had to pray to the house of choice that was given to me, while mixing with people who looked down on others and felt better than them because of certain reasons of their given clothing. I was told God made us more special, and that seemed unfair.

Home became very ugly. Mum would scream about Dad and spit poison to us about him. And, when my brothers and I were with Dad, he and his new girlfriend would joke about my mother in a spiteful school playground way. Both sides were trying to win and be better. I wrote letters that my father asked me to write. Then, a few weeks later, my mother would scream and shout while waving the very letter saying how my dad had used them against her in court. Both would tell me and my brothers lies about the other. I was being torn apart, and no one seemed to care. For some reason, my brothers and I were not enemies in this battle but found ourselves dealing with it all on our own. Looking back, it would have been nice to know we shared the same pain. But we were so hurt that we dared not tell each other. Our own secrets, in our separate misery, of our joined life. It's like we had our own special bunkers, and there was no way to speak of how we each really felt. Mum and Dad seemed to enjoy their hate and saw nothing of our hurt. This became extra clothing. A thick coat, gloves and scarf, on top of the already odd-fitting ones. It became very stuffy. Secretly, I wanted to take it all off. To run bare and naked, like when I was born, and find some new clothes. Some that would fit me the way I wanted. But how could I? They were what I was supposed to wear, and to think differently would make me bad. Bad fitting clothes, sewn down with the force of guilt and fear. Do this and get this. Be this and get that. Don't and you won't. I remember a feeling of just wanting everyone to be together again and happy, even though I could never actually remember it that way. Of course, I always had Sunny to spend times in the garden with, or in the woods next door. He was my best friend. We dug for bones, played with my soldiers, and enjoyed the sandpit at the back of the garden. Anyway, one day, after another bombardment of loud screams from Mum about Dad, I decided to head off to the woods. I had no time to think of taking Sunny. I just ran out the back door to the end of the garden to get away from the war. I climbed up the twisted tree near the fence and clumsily, slid over and into the freedom place where the weight and my uncomfortable clothes just vanished.

Once over the fence, the woods became my other place away from it all. Like a hidden forest. One minute, I was in the war, escaping the enemy; the next, I was a wolf chasing deer, running at full speed through trees and bushes with no care for the scratches from the thorns and tree branches. I howled and got on my hands and knees and bounced forward and then hunched down, ready to attack. My imagination was free. My clothes did not exist. The war at home was so far away that I never even thought of it. The stream that ran through the wood was also a great enjoyment for me. I enjoyed breaking my grubby nails, pulling rocks out of the clay mud to make dams, and then sticking my fingers deep into that clay to use it as filler in between the rocks. I saw myself as a fully qualified engineer. No leaks and perfectly strong. I was an artist at dam building. The clay was even sculptured to smooth the walls. But, of course, after the water level had risen to its near overflow height, the soon-to-be downfall of the dam became a way to let out some hidden pain. The perfect picture of hydro structure was then bombed with rocks at high speed to break its perfect design. I watched the drips grow stronger and stronger with great excitement until the clay just moved and cracked and then burst as the water found its freedom. The pain seemed to ease when the water was released.

Not long after the dam had been destroyed, as I sat watching the water end its escape and find its calm flow again, I sensed someone around me. I looked, but no one was there. The feeling seemed to grow. I started to feel like I was a soldier, lost and tired, unsure and afraid, away from the safety of his battalion. I spun around again and again. My heart was pounding, and my whole body became stiff. I started to head up the wooded hill, away from the stream and towards home. The sense grew stronger as my sprint became that of a mountain lion running away from the danger of man. Maybe I found this animal in my imagination to stop the fear and feel bolder? As I turned to see if anyone was following me, I tripped over a tree root sticking up through the fallen leaves. In slow motion, I went down, face-first into the dirt. Because I was winded, I forgot my fear for a few seconds. Then, I felt it again. I looked all around me. No one.

" Who's there?" I shouted, trying to be brave.

I became warm. Something very comfortable came over me. My fear seemed to fade. Something was near. Then, from inside and outside, from all around and up and down, a voice came to me. It was everyone's voice and no one's. The fear had now gone and been replaced by a sudden peace.

" Hello, you. It's all going to be wonderful, I promise," said the voice.

And, for some reason, I believed his words.

"Who are you? Where are you?" I asked quietly.

"Let's just say that I am Him. Where am I? I'm in the trees. I'm in the leaves. I'm in the ants, and I'm in the streams."

"Really?" I asked, a little unsure.

"You can doubt me if you like. That is your choice," said Him.

I managed to stand up and brush myself off. Some leaves fell off my clothes. But they did something very strange. They fell upwards. I felt for the wind, but there was none.

"Are you a wizard?" I asked with a hopeful smile.

"I am, if you want me to be," he said.

"I think I have to go. It's nearly tea time," I explained, nervously.

"I know. I will meet with you again, sometime soon," Him said, calmly.

"You will?" I asked.

There was no reply, but I noticed the woods around me. I noticed the cold, and the noise of the air under the crow's wings as it flew past. Everything was now very much there, when before it seemed to all blend into, well, into nothing. I quickly fell back into my fully clothed me, panicked, with a head full of everything and anything. I started to run for the garden fence as quickly as I could. As I ran, I turned. There was no one there, but I felt a small smile find my face as my clothes vanished again for a split second. Then, I turned on the run and headed home.

CHAPTER TWO

I was upstairs with Sunny, telling him all about Him, when my brother came into the room.

"Do you believe in wizards?" I asked.

"Don't be stupid," he said. And he pushed past, grabbed something, and walked off. He always called everything and everyone stupid. Maybe, if he was the best at school, I might agree with him, but he was a little less smart and a little more stupid than me. But I never returned fire on his attacks.

Sunny and I ran down the stairs to the dinner table. Both my brothers were sitting, waiting. Of course, there were no knives or forks or glasses on the table, let alone the jug of Orange Squash. I guess, as usual, I would volunteer. I walked into the kitchen and noticed my mum quickly cover up her tears. She turned and smiled and gave me a nice hug, a real, long, hug. Like she needed something from me, and not the normal other way round, hug.

"Do you believe in wizards, Mum?" I asked.

"Only wizard solicitors who can squeeze the blood of money out of the stone that is your slime of a father," she answered very angrily.

I made the smart choice to end my talk right there and get on with my duties. I decided to keep Him a secret for now. My very own wizard, I thought. For some reason, his words kept coming back to me. Not in my head, but all around, inside and out.

"It's all going to be wonderful. I promise."

I wish it were right now. My brothers would pinch me and punch me when mum was not looking, and I would never tell. I knew the future would be full of the same punishment for doing so. One of my brothers began to stretch the truth and become a terrible liar as well as calling everyone stupid, and he seemed to do it more and more, even though he was constantly proved to be wrong. And Mum used to always say that, if you keep calling everyone stupid, you will end up that way. My other brother was the brightest of us all.

He was not so bad to me, but he did think that, because of his age, he deserved respect and thought he was of course better than me at everything, even if it was obvious he was not. He seemed to be just as lost in his head as I was, but I never asked if he also did not like his clothes.

The next day, I had to put on my least liked clothes. I had to go to Sunday school, Hebrew classes. I always asked about the time before man wrote his stories in a book, and I was pinched and had my hair pulled by the rabbi. This is religion? It felt like the war at home. I had to learn to read Hebrew writing, but had no idea what I was reading. I tried to question why I learned French at school and got to understand it, but not here. Again I got bullied into silence. Like those soldiers in the war movies who were evil and nasty when they captured someone from the other side. But they were being beaten to get information. I was being beaten to be quiet. Why did I have to wear a hat inside and not outside, and yet some did both? Why did I have to just go to one building if God was so almighty? And if he could split himself into different buildings, could he not be everywhere in between? Each question got a nasty and horrible answer with a hand. Later, at the quick, early end of my time in Hebrew classes, the war would be won against this enemy, but that is another story, and a story quite shocking.

As soon as the bell would ring and I could get out of the building, the clothes would fall off instantly. I was free again. I liked my walk back from Sunday school. It was like no man's land. Not like the woods. They were real freedom. Not like Sunny, he was real truth and real love. Not like the love I knew from people. The human-to-human love had so many clouds and twists to it. There was anger, blackmail, guilt, and pressure. Anyway, I enjoyed my street walk home after battling the cruel rabbi. Every now and then, my other brother, the middle one, would join me instead of being with his friends. He was always different to me on that walk, always nicer. Maybe he also liked the free time away from the ill-fitting clothes of others. But that was a little too heavy for us to be talking about. We would just enjoy being with each other in a way we liked, without treading on minefields. But I knew he did not like the clothes of others, like me. He wanted peace inside, also. He always wanted peace. I knew this. We got home, and he put on his big brother clothes, and our truth vanished as the front door closed. Sunny ran up to greet me, and my life glowed. I told him of the silliness of it all, and he laughed and told me everything would be wonderful. He did, but he did not need to speak. And I suddenly realized that his voice was the same as Him, and Him as Sunny. Him, I missed him. I wondered when he would return.

Anyway, today was Dad day. And that was another part of the uncomfortable clothing. But it also had some good things wrapped around the silliness of it all. Mum would keep Dad waiting outside, as she knew his temper would boil. She enjoyed pulling the big red curtains in the front room, knowing he would see her doing it. Then, she just kept us back. This would, of course, bring anger from Dad about how she does it on purpose. But it would also bring one of the good things in his way of trying to better himself to get back at her.

"What's your mum give you for pocket money?" he would ask.

Now, knowing he was going to try and be better than her, I would, being of a clever mind, use this to get some payment for being in a war I had no choice in. I would tell my dad a little white lie and say Mum was giving me more than she actually was, so he would, of course, up his money by a stupid amount to become bigger and better than her and try and buy our love which, in some ways, he did.

Mum came from a richer family than Dad, but Dad started to do well in business and always had a big bundle of cash on him. He wore gold chains and drove a big flashy American car. No one had them back then in London. Everyone would look at us and my Dad loved it. Even though it was another kind of clothing, I did secretly like it. And being able to be in the front seat, on my turn, was like being royalty. I would have the window down and use the electric seat to raise me up, so I could lean my arm on the window ledge. This was kind of like fame. Not all clothes felt bad. But it was not real and never lasted, and, from what I was reminded, always costs a lot of money to keep the show a show.

Another war used against us was the clothes we wore. Our real clothes. Mum, even though she came from a better background, was never flashy. She was very real and down-to-earth. She never felt like she had to wear labeled clothes to feel better. I loved that about her. Even though she was of a better class, as she always reminded us, she did not believe in one of the biggest lies of it all. To spend a lot of money, to wear something that cost far less, to seem to be something bigger. But my dad was always proud of the silly amount of money he would spend on a shirt or trousers, and he spoke loudly of the brand name and label that they had. Anyway, my dad hated my mother's way with real clothes because we were all very much like her. We would wear our clothes and get in the car and the first thing my dad would do was attack my mum for allowing us to go out dressed like that.

"I can't take you out to eat looking like that! She dresses you like council estate kids!" he shouted.

This name calling had also become a way to get some kind of payback for being in their war. I would wear ripped jeans and say everything was still in the laundry basket because Mum had not done the laundry yet. I got him angry with her for wearing bad clothes, so he would try and better her again and take us out and spoil us with new clothes. There were those moments, as my dad was paying for the new smart clothes at the shop counter, when my brothers and I shared fond happy memories of our winnings and treasures of the war. We would stand behind him, all fancy panted up with smiles at our success. Being three boys, we would take turns in who would be the bad dresser. Then all smart, it would be a nice Italian or French restaurant where we would meet his soon-to-be new wife, who I really liked. She did not care about swearing around us and smoked one cigarette after the other. My dad would always say the same thing every time:"You're like a chimney, you are."

And she would say, "And you sound like a broken record."

We all laughed, every time. These were fun moments. But they were also covered in the fact that Mum would be angry with us for at least a day after the visit. And, of course, Dad and his lady would spit jokes and bad words at us about Mum. But the fact that they were not two-faced about saying swear words and that they let it all out made me feel happy that not all adults lived that lie. We all cursed at school, or with our friends and brothers, just like they did when they were kids. But Mum would beat us for saying the smallest bad word, and then, when in the car, she would call the driver in front of us a fucking Paki or Arab or other bad things, even if they were white. That clothing lie was not nice and never made sense. I was well brought up enough to know when and where I could use bad language. Parents, parenting like their parents, even though they did not like being parented that way. I always felt like I was being treated like a fool.

So, Dad day was a bonus in two ways. In money, which gave me a feeling of being better and bigger, and, in actual clothes, as they were also of a labeled, overpriced quality. I was now driving a big car with a bundle of cash. I was wearing my dad's clothes. And my mother hated it.

"How much did he give you?" she asked with anger, as I walked in the house.

And now the inside out, back to front had to happen. I would have to hide some of the money so as not to annoy her too much, or she would call Dad and go mad. I had to lie about the lie I had given to get the money I got. She was already mad just about us seeing our Dad. Mum was always upset at things. I think they called it stress and worry. But she did have her moments of joy. And she became the most beautiful lady in the world when she did.

There was now a new man in her life, and he seemed to be around a lot but kept very quiet and calm all the time. He made sure our business was not his, and it seemed to work. I did respect him for that, although sometimes his calm ways would have been liked over my mother's temper when it came to punishment. Not that sometimes I did not ask for it, but we were beaten with a wooden spoon. I remember once running away with my hands behind my back, covering my bum, so Mum could not hit it with the spoon. But then my fingers got hit, and I moved my hands away to avoid more pain, only to leave the target wide open, which then got hit, and so my hurting hands went straight back to protect it. But, one day—and it was an incredible moment—the spoon, in all its terror, broke. The enemy, like that emperor, had no clothes on. Mum had no weapon. Would she dare use actual skin against skin? I turned and faced her, and, to my amazement, Mum backed away. Like all her power was gone. I was a seven-foot tall child. I was a David against her Goliath.

Anyway. After coming back from Dad and not wanting to be a part of the huge ugliness that always followed, I decided to take Sunny to the woods. I will walk the dog and get brownie points to bring me back to a happy place with Mum, I thought. I wondered how lucky I was to have the woods next door. I get to be in nature away from the wars and clothes as much as I like, I thought. And then I thought that it must be more natural to be in nature, free from the weight of the clothes of everything. Everyone was so busy worrying about what others thought, and this made them try so hard to make sure they were thought well of. They clothed themselves with lie on top of lie, to live a lie, to feel good in others' eyes. Well, this is how I saw it, like a prison of what others thought. There seemed to be a fear to take off the clothes which I then saw I also had about mine. But mine was the fear of survival, not of what others thought. I was too small to go out and earn money, and I only had one home, and I had to live by the rules, wear their clothes.

As soon as I got in the woods, I imagined being a caveman before the time that we know about, and it seemed no one then had clothes of any type. Everyone was probably just equal and truthful. I was not ready to be naked for real. I did not ask to be born. I did not make a choice as to whom would dress me, yet here I was under others' orders, doing what others thought was right for me without being asked what I wanted or thought. I won't do this to my kids if I have them, I thought. I think cavemen must have been much happier than most people these days. I wonder if the African people who live in the jungles still have extra things put on them by others? We got a hundred yards into the wood, and it was time to free Sunny. Even he had to wear something to be controlled. When I took off the leash, it would be like watching me in him. He was off, running through the trees chasing squirrels. I imagined him imagining like I did. Was he thinking he was a wolf, also? Maybe he was even a tiger in India.

On the path in the woods, there would always be other people now and then with their dogs, and I would see them and quickly move off the path and into the wood out of shyness. I don't actually know why I even stuck to the path. It was always uncomfortable, and I always felt better leaving it. It was also something I had to do. Stay on the path. Do as you're told. Stay off the grass, the signs always said. That's how I saw everyone. Walking on a cement path, all clothed in neat long lines. And I wanted to be naked, dancing on the grass. Well, I was free to do as I pleased in the wood, and I did. I soon became a bold wolf and started to chase Sunny. Whoever he was in his mind did not matter because we seemed to be doing the same thing, playing the same game. He ran ahead of me, jumping logs, and I followed. He would turn to see if I made it okay. Then I would be in front of him, and he would enjoy the chase, which made me feel like I was a super hero wolf with extra speed and strength. Time would change for me when I would play with Sunny like this. I would jump in slow motion and then run faster than a horse. Sometimes when I would jump, I felt like I could fly, and it really was quite real to me. Maybe it was. This time of no time and no weight of clothing was better than ice cream and chocolate. It was better than Christmas. That's another silly thing. We were Jewish, but Mum loved Christmas. It was very confusing to have to wear odd-fitting clothes that don't fit each other. Like wearing a coat in summer time. Or putting a sock on your hand and then a glove over that sock.

Eventually, I would trip and roll into a heap covered in mud and leaves. Sunny would jump onto me like a lion, and we would tumble and roll for a while. Nothing was needed here, and everything was happy. Then it happened again. And Sunny sensed it also. I knew now and waited with excitement for his first words. I looked around but knew Him was nowhere and everywhere. I smiled and looked down at Sunny who seemed to smile back. He knows Him already, I think.

"The clothes of others will go away, if you wish them to," Him said. "Like leaving the path in the woods, you can take them off."

"How did you know about that?" I asked. There was silence. The world seemed to have a knowing smile.

"But what will happen if I do that?" I asked.

"If you have the courage to do it, you will find the courage to face the words of war to try and get you to dress in them again. "

As I looked up, I suddenly found myself looking down at me looking up. Yet, the me on the ground could not see this me. For a moment or two, which felt like forever, I became what seemed to be and felt like the universe. I was Him. I was me. I was Sunny. I was the sky and the sun and the space that always seems to be nothing but actually had more to it than everything else. This, I imagined, could be what they say is heaven. It seemed that every question in the world was answered in a second. Then, within a second, I was back looking up at nothing. I looked down at Sunny who just smiled at me. Everything was alive. Not nature alive but even the spaces in nature. Everything seemed to be one thing. Everything was connected like a huge invisible Legoland. Emptiness is not what we think or ignore it to be, I thought. It is the glue to it all.

"What was that? What did you do?" I said.

"You are nothing that you think you are, and far more than you could possibly think," Him said.

The world seemed to smile at me again, and Him was gone. I smiled back. I looked around, and I laughed. I had been given a key to the treasure box of it all. Nothing could stop me now. I was totally indestructible. Little did I know that I would fall very quickly back into the clothes of others, and my power in the woods would vanish as quickly as it came to me. As I walked in the house, I was met straight away with a scream of "Take your boots off!" Yet Sunny walked right in with muddy paws. I knew what I had to do. But mum's scream beat me to it. The nonsense of it all started, and I did as I was told. I did have a thought of courage to speak up, speak the sense, but life just swallowed me up like a big dark rabbit hole. Being a child, dressed by others who thought they knew what was best for me, was not very comfortable. It seems that adults grow up and forget what it feels like to be a child, and then they become what they did not like. I tried to hold onto what I felt in the woods, but it faded very fast. It was like I was drifting asleep from my waking.

"I know what's best for you!" And "Do you know how much it costs to send you to a good school? " Then, on top of that. " You should be proud to be Jewish." And the cherry on the guilt cake: "Do you know how much I have to sacrifice for you boys?" The whips of words of the jailer of my own home prison life. I think Mum was letting her anger at Dad and life out on us. I didn't understand when she had a new man why she was still so angry, but it continued. It was like she was carrying all this stuff inside that was always boiling and bubbling. I guess it rubbed off because I got thrown out of Cub Scouts for an angry incident. These incidents seem to follow me through my younger life. Authority was like the Germans in the war movies. From very young, I believed no human had a right to tell another what to do. Everyone had their ideas for me, and no one allowed or even cared to hear my own voice. There seemed to be a lot of guilt, blackmail, and fear in life to keep control. Home, school, and especially Sunday school.

Anyway. It was the end of the week. I came in from school, walked in from the front door, and ran into the morning room to see Sunny. He wagged his tail but did not rush up to meet me. Mum was standing there with a soft face, for a change. I gave Sunny a hug, and he melted into me with love. This was virtually the same feeling as when I was with Him, up in the air. Nothing was wrong and everything was amazing. Then, Mum got down and sat with Sunny and me and started to tell me that she had gone to the vet because there was a lump in his side. She said they did some tests and they will know in about a week. I looked at Sunny who seemed to understand. He was calm. Mum ran her fingers through my hair, and she lay down with me. This was one of those special moments when Mum became my cotton wool blanket. She seemed to forget all the pain and enjoyed Sunny as much as I did. She had forgotten how much one can get from a dog by simply laying down and loving it. My brother came in from school and saw us all on the floor.

"Sunny is sick, and the vet is doing some tests," I said.

My brother seemed to lose his clothes of toughness as he sat down on the floor with us.

Even though this was not a fun time, this was a time we all left the other life to one side and found family again. My brother found Sunny's funny spot, and he tickled him and made his leg kick. Then, he started singing a tune to it, from a popular song in the charts at the time. Mum joined in. "In the summertime when the weather is fine, you can reach up high and touch the sky..."

Me and Mum laughed, and Sunny smiled like a crazy dog. Good medicine for all of us. Then, the phone rang, and it was like the bell for another round of boxing as soon as Mum picked it up. I grabbed the dog's lead and showed it to Mum, to ask if it was okay. She waved her hand and scowled her face as if to say, "Yes, yes, go on." Sunny was fine, no real difference, just a little tired from the adventure of going to the vet in the car. We walked out the house, down the street, and into the woods. As I walked in, I wondered if I would meet Him again. I looked around with such focus that everything really did seem to be connected. I was standing to attention with my attention. I was wide awake, clothing off, and the dial turned up to full. Sunny was unclipped and off he went. I think the woods gave him some fresh energy. I followed him as quickly as I could. We ran down to the stream in and out of the trees like soldiers or spies on a mission. When we got there, three kids were hanging around. One was up a tree, and two others were on the ground, watching. The one up the tree, about six feet up, had a frog, and he was dropping it onto the ground. The others were laughing. At least, the ground was padded with leaves and mud, but I am sure the frog was not happy. Then one of the kids jumped into the stream and got a big rock. I stood there and watched him put it under the tree. I spoke up.

"Come on. Don't hurt it. What's it done to you? Leave it alone."

The kid in the tree told to me to shut up as the rock was put under him. It was too late. He dropped the frog, and it hit the rock with a thud. I think I cried instantly. I went to get the frog, and the other two tried to stop me, but Sunny stepped in and growled. The other boy climbed down and was also kept back by my bodyguard. They laughed a not so funny laugh and backed away and called me names well into the distance. The frog had split and was about as close to being dead as I could imagine. His little open body seemed to be gasping, gripping to survive. Then, without thought, I picked up the big rock and squashed it.

As soon as it hit, I woke from the trance of what I had just done.

I wanted to be a vet, but I did not think I could put dogs to sleep to stop the pain. But here I was ending the last pains of a frog. It was like I was being told to do this from somewhere. I spun around. But Him was nowhere. But then he never was. Sunny sniffed the rock and looked at me. It had to be done. I kept thinking, Why do I not feel bad? I even tried to feel guilty, but it just seemed right. I now sensed that sense of Him, but it was like he was walking with us quietly. I looked up and smiled.

"I know you're here," I said.

Then, Him spoke. But again, it was inside and outside, not my ears that heard
it. It was a knowing of a voice.

"I'm always with you and everyone else, everywhere," him said.

"Then why are you speaking to me?" I replied.

"Who is speaking? And who says I don't speak to everyone else, also?

"Who else do you speak to?" I asked.

"You like the idea of the spoken word. Do I have lips? Are you hearing me or knowing me?" he answered. And I sensed a big smile. "Apple," he said.

"Apple?" I questioned.

"You label and signpost everything with words. Yet, a word is not what it is, is it?"

"It isn't? "I replied.

"An apple could be called a table. It is the experience that counts. Before one eats it and tastes it, it is what it is, and no label will really give you what it actually is. Once tasted, it becomes real, experienced. Anything else is just a label. Or, as you call it, clothing."

I smiled. He was all of me, and I was all of Him. I was having a talk with myself, and I don't actually think I was talking.

"No creature requires a signpost but understands the world around them because they have not narrowed it down to words. They know. They experience. People experience through dreams and daydreams, as you are now. People write what comes to them, and we read those experiences. Some, over time, write when they have not experienced and pretend. These words have caused a lot of trouble with the clothing of man over the years, causing much guilt and fear. But that's okay because, it's always going to be wonderful. Art, music, books, film all come from the same place," he explained.

I looked around and saw everything without a label. I saw everything as Sunny would see it, or a bird. It all was what it was, and all part of a picture and not separate. I also felt part of it all. These clothes fit nicely. In fact, I was not really wearing anything. This is the naked truth of it all. Not a wood. Not dangerous. Not muddy. Not wet. Not the named season or a time of day or anything else a word could explain. If you think about everything that way, it really does change things. Layers and layers of history and time and clothing that grew and grew and kept this knowing far away. As I was looking around and seeing, or should I say knowing everything, I also knew Him was not there anymore. Even though he was. It's not anything I can put into words. It's like the time before words, yet in this time. Being silent with it all was something that never really happens in life. My mind was quiet and all clothes had gone. It was like a quiet hug with life. I put the lead on Sunny, and we walked home just as the rain started to fall. I just let it rain on me. No fear or worry of what Mum would say coming home wet. No fear of being wet or getting cold. They were all silly words of fear in my mind. Silliness put onto me by others, and them by others before them. A history of hand-me-down, fearful clothing that seemed to squash the true life out of life. As I got to the front door, Mum was there, waiting.

"Look at you. I was worried. You will catch a cold. You're all wet," she said.

"No, I won't, Mum. It's all going to be wonderful," I said.

And I looked at Mum, and she actually believed me for a second. She dropped her face of fears and smiled but only for a second or two.

"Go and have a warm bath but dry the dog off first," she said softly.

Sunny liked this part. I would do what Grandma would do when we came out the bath, when we were younger. The Rubadubdub. I think Sunny knew when it was going to rain because he would bark to go out just to get wet, and come back in for drying and sing song. It was a good day in the life of me. Very little clothes, and not much war. Sunny, the woods, and Him. I tried again to feel sad for the frog, but it seemed to all be okay, for some reason.

Later in my life, this happened a few times with animals. Once, while on holiday, walking on a desert road, in Israel, towards the border with

Egypt, I had a daydream in my head of a bird injured on the side of the road. Like the frog, I just picked up a rock and ended its pain. I snapped out of my daydream and shook off the horrible feeling. But then, five minutes later, further up the road, an actual bird lay on the side of the road, flapping, broken, in pain. Without thought, I did what was told to me in the dream. After, I tried to find guilt or sadness, but it was meant to be.

Anyway, I was in bed, clean, dry, and comfortable. Mum left the door open, so I could see some light. Really, I just wanted to be able to hear others in the house and know I was okay before my brother had his bedtime, because we shared a bedroom. I don't know why I felt lonely, but I found going to bed like that. I was never tired.

CHAPTER THREE

My walk to school was like the walk back from Sunday class. A wonderful freedom in between adults who thought they knew what was best for me. I did not have much time left at this school, as I was going to go to another. I was told it was a better one. I was reminded of how much it would cost to send me there. Was this just a Jewish thing with the reminding of money and the cost of everything, or did everyone put that weight on their children? If I knew I could make a choice and not cost them the money, it might be a less heavy life with less clothing. But I had no say.

I knew I was not brilliant at school, but I also knew most of those who were had no sense out of school. I wondered why no adults did school work, but they used sense. It all made no sense to me. I saw, from a young age, that unless I was to be a scientist or a doctor, or something like that, it was all a waste for me. Was anything I learned going to be used in my life? There was nothing about life. No life lessons. It's like a prison term for machines being programmed with useless information, learning to sit in lines, stand in lines, and walk the line. To obey the authority. It was like we were being trained like dogs. Was all the history, geography, and crazy math of shapes and angles going to be used throughout my life? The fact that my mother had no idea when I asked her about those things made me think, Why do I need to know this? From a young age, I thought, if I learn it and don't use it, it's kind of like useless and a waste. I knew I wanted to either be a vet or a stunt man or James Bond. But I wanted to have fun and enjoy my life. Whenever any adults would speak of their day, they would moan and complain of the traffic and their work, and they never had a good thing to say about their job and their life. So I decided earlier in life that in later life I would play as much as I could and love my life and not moan and complain about work. This, my mother told me, was crazy.

"You have to work. You have to have responsibilities, and life is not easy." She would repeat that again and again. It was like people did hypnosis on their own lives. Telling them that life is unhappy all the time. I kept my clothes on and did not argue with her about it. I did not say I did not want to grow up and be miserable like everyone else.

"When I grow up, I'm going to do what I want, when I want. And that way I will always be happy!" I shouted at Mum.

"Well, not while you are living under my roof," was her quick prison guard answer.

This was the secret dream that I wanted to make come true. To live doing as I wanted when I wanted. To play.

Adults always looked forward to the weekend, to end their week. And always wanted to go away on holiday to escape their life of work. There was always something up ahead better than where they were. It was like, once the weekend came, life was nice. When they went on holiday, life was nice. There was too much not nice and too little nice in a life for adults. I am glad I had the thoughts I did at a young age. I knew I was going to do something I loved and something that was such fun that I never worked, ever, and never wanted to complain or get away from my life.

Anyway, the always fitting into the clothes of everyone else started to become a prison of rules and ideas and ways to think and how to be and what to be. It was like everyone was being brainwashed out of their real self and into something smartly controlled by very smart people. Every now and then, Him's words would echo through my body, and I would smile at the lie of it all because I really did know he was right about it all being wonderful. Everyone around me was always worried about something. And then, as always that something always worked out. It was like everyone was frightened all the time. I was becoming different. Like I was looking at everyone in a goldfish bowl. I tried sometimes to speak up, but was either pinched by the rabbi, laughed at by my brothers, shouted at by my mother, or punished at school. Was I the problem, or was everyone else stuck in a nightmare? My time with Him had made me a little more awake then before. I knew. I had special inside information. I saw the madness of it all. Yet, much of the time, I had to play the play, live the lie, wear the clothes of others to keep those who kept me happy. The guilt to be what I wanted to be was backed up by the fear of not being what they wanted me to be. A very smart, clever control system to keep people clothed. It was funny. God had not struck anyone down with lightning for as long as I could remember or I had heard of, so that silliness did not work on me. I had no fear of an almighty. What religion was he, anyway? And if he had none, why did I have to have one? Who was God's choice of god, and was he allowed a choice? Who called him God? Did he say call me this? So many questions about something no one could actually prove. And I thought about it, if one religion could prove that their god was the right god, the only god, then surely all the other religions would fall down? The mystery that had everyone divided up and hating and fighting. It all made no sense to me.

Meeting Him allowed me to see things differently. It was like a light got switched on. I knew about treating people the same way I wanted to be treated, which I had heard was the golden rule, which I think was the way that all problems would be solved in the world. I knew about not doing bad. But then one of my influences of the opposite was my Dad. He would speak and boast of his violence. Once, when I was with my brothers and my dad's new wife in the car, we were at the gate to get out of his block of flats, in the underground car park, and the black man on the gate was arguing with him about something. My dad got out the car and slammed him onto the bonnet, and then punched the man again and again. After putting the man aside and opening the arm of the gate, he got into the car feeling like a gladiator and bragged how he taught him a lesson and that no one should get on his wrong side. I knew this was very wrong, and it was very ugly to see and very frightening, but there was also some of that rubbing off onto me. I could be like that. I could be like my dad. I was clothing myself in my dad's temper, and I did not know it. I also had my mum's anger and temper. The clothes of our parents' ways and words become part of us through some form of secret transfer. When I was not in my awake mind, I became like my mother in an uneasy, angry mind inside my head. I felt tense and nervous over nothing and everything. And then sometimes I would have rage come to the surface and break things and smash whatever I could, like the dam I built and broke again and again. It was like part of the smart trick to keep us all on a hamster wheel of acting the same as our parents, and them before. I was fighting inside my head. A prisoner of me and my clothes.

CHAPTER FOUR

I was waking up more and more. I seemed to be happy for no actual reason. Not always, but often. The next time I met Him was somewhere totally different. Obviously, he was not tied to the woods, but I never thought I would meet him where I did.

I was walking home from school in my daydreaming head. Something caught my eye on the ground, and I bent down and picked it up. I turned it around and there, as I had learned, was a hallmark. I had just found a gold watch laying in the gutter. I held it in my open hand to feel its weight. The two tests to know if it was real gold or not. And it was heavy for its size, for sure. I was so excited. I wanted to tell my mum as quick as I could, and back up the street, just about ten yards, was a phone box. I could have just walked on for another ten minutes and got home to show my mum my treasure, but I made the choice to go back and go into the big red phone box and call. Life, it seemed, could have different roads that could bring about totally different stories. I scrambled for change in my pocket and put the two pence piece in the slot. I put my finger in the first number and excitedly waited for it to wind back for the next. In those days, we had no buttons. Everything had a round dial. Even the television. All of a sudden, I felt a huge draft of air on the back of my neck, and I turned around to see the door open and four boys, all bigger than me, from the estates down the road, standing, blocking the door. One of them grabbed me, and I dropped the phone. He punched me straight in the cheek and pulled me out onto the pavement. Before I could think, I put my hand in my pocket and screamed, "I found a gold watch! Take it!"

As the boy raised his fist to hit me again, he stopped. Another grabbed the watch, and the boy let go of me and grabbed the watch back.

"It's real. It's got a hallmark. Take it."

The boy turned it around and then, as I had, held the weight in his open hand. I don't know how we both knew of these things. Maybe from a movie or TV. But thank God he knew what I knew. He smiled at his easy treasure and let go of me. Now he was happy and all the others wanted to see, and he was trying to keep the vultures off. I got up, like a frightened sheep, but, as I did, the bigger boy with the watch turned around. He looked at me for a second.

"Get out of here," he said.

I thought, If I had just walked on, I could be home by now and have a gold watch to sell. If only I had waited. If only I had not gone into the phone box. And then, while my mind was going crazy, Him smiled. He smiled, and I felt it. He spoke, and I experienced it without words or without hearing. He showed me the other way to see it. I had no gold watch, and I still have no gold watch. If I did not have the gold watch, I might have been punched a lot more than I was, if I met the kids in the street. I was saved by the very thing that made me change my journey to get attacked. I actually laughed out loud. I looked up and around.

"Life will bring accidents and many other bad things, but it is how we see them and what they can teach us that is important. There is always a lesson that will strengthen us if we look right.

Things will always pass through our lives and never stay the same. There is strength to be found in the bad and good things in life. Don't hang onto the good or worry about the bad. Neither of them stay bad or good for long. They fade, and life always continues," he said.

I don't think anyone had ever been punched and robbed and felt so good about it. I was still alive and had lost nothing from before I found the watch, but I did learn not to become the bad in my mind. I lost the sadness of it all. I decided not to tell my mum or anyone the story. I would just say that I fell on the way home and bruised my face, falling off a wall which, in the end, got me a nice extra cookie and a hug from Mum. Most of the time, I would be so squashed by the clothes of others and trying to be what others wanted, that I would forget the madness of it all. But then the moments would come, and I would just smile. My body would relax, and life seemed to go speeding around me as if I was in a slow motion protected ball. It will be very nice to meet someone one day who also knows Him, like I do, I thought. Then we can laugh at all of it together. It's always nice to share the good things.

Well, some don't. How some people could

have so much money and not give and help more people always made me wonder what it was about money that made people so greedy. Maybe they were frightened it would go away, or they would not have enough. But my brother explained to me how interest worked in the bank and how people bought buildings and shops and got rent and that meant that, even if they did not work anymore, they would always earn money from their money.

I did the sums, and it was quite crazy how much people could make from just doing nothing when they had so much, and they still worked and stressed. They had big houses and big boats and lots of cars and lots to pay to look after it all, so they had to keep earning to pay for their big life. It seemed like a stress to have to keep up all the time. In my perfect world, after a certain amount of money anyone made, the rest would have to go back to everyone else for the good of all. I thought, if everyone was looked after by everyone else, then everyone else would look after everyone, and no one would want to hurt or rob from others, so others would not fear being hurt or robbed. It might not be good for the burglary alarm business, but I am sure they would find something else to do. And maybe the poor kids from the estate who punched me would not have done it, and I would have a gold watch. Oh, well.

My grandpa, who now lived in Spain, did well in business, but he never had a need to be showy or flashy, like my dad. He always told the story of where he came from and how he got to where he was. But unlike most, with not even that much money, he never cared to wear it, drive it, or overspend. He told us he was so poor when he was young that he would go to school one day and his brother the next because they only had one pair of shoes. And the school was so poor that there were no pencils or paper. They had sandboxes on their desks and would write in the sand with their fingers, then wipe it away. He also told how he had to leave school at fourteen to go to work because his dad fell ill, and he had six brothers and sisters to help look after. He worked for the milkman back in the day when it was a horse and cart. As my grandpa ran the milk bottles from the cart to the front door, the milkman would just sit holding the leather reins as the horse slowly walked up the street. It was a job of constant keep up. And at the end of the week, when he got his few pennies in his hand, he said he felt like a millionaire. In fact, he said, later in life, nothing ever matched that feeling, no matter how well he did. Anyway. I loved him very much. He was always funny and always had amazing stories to tell. Everyone would listen to him when he would come over for a visit. I sometimes wondered if maybe he had met Him, once. He seemed to know more about life than most. When we would finish our main meal, when out to eat, he would say, "Hands up, all those who don't want ice cream." And, of course, we would all put our hands up and fall for it. We laughed every time. In fact, we laughed a lot around Grandpa. And Mum also seemed to find a lot of peace when he was around. She was a little girl again, not angry at my dad. Grandpa had a nice flat in Majorca that overlooked the sea. He lived with his second wife, who was a little strict and grumpy to us, but she did love him, and they were sweet. He said he retired early and lived small, so he could live a longer, less stressful life. It seemed to make more sense than the always needing to work to pay for the big life.

CHAPTER FIVE

The effects of Him never lasted very long after our meetings, but it sat inside me, in my mind, making a stew of being awake, and somehow being smarter than I was before. Maybe this is where wisdom comes from?

My mother always worried. Everything was a stress. And then add onto this, the anger she always carried about my dad. It made her quite an unhappy person. She was also always complaining about everyone else, everywhere. She was very well brought up, she always told me, and most people were not. This was an item of clothing that also did not fit too well. But I began to take on my mother's reactions to the world and so, on top of my life in general, the war, the clothes, I had a constant unease about everything and everyone. Of course, the moments of being clear would burst through, but they would drown in the madness very quickly. I was two people in one. The clear, awake me and the fast asleep, clothed me who started becoming my parent's ways.

My big brothers were too busy being big brothers for me to be able to be a friend to them. At nights I lay down in the lounge on the floor with Sunny as my mum watched the TV with her man. They always smiled as they watched us play. Sunny never worried. His only stress was when it was close to dinner time and he couldn't get his food any quicker than he wanted it. Anyway, soon enough, it was time to go up stairs to bed. I did wonder if Him would come to me while I drifted off, but he never did. I'm glad actually, because I might have thought he was a dream, or I could even have forgotten that he had come at all.

At school the next day, the subject of religions came up, and I heard for the first time of a man called Buddha. He was once a rich prince who was unhappy with the world and walked away from his riches and wondered off with nothing, just to find wisdom and real happiness. I liked this story. Even a rich prince did not like his clothes. They named him the Buddha, which meant the enlightened one, and his wandering lessons became a religion, kind of. Some say it was just a way of life. I decided I wanted to learn more about this man and what he found out about life without his clothes. From my secret library visits, I read that they even thought many hundreds of years after the prince died, another man who went wondering for many years and returned very wise could have found this way of life and brought it back to another part of the world. But that part of his life, the time he went missing, in all the books about him, was empty. It made no sense. The most famous man in the world, and a huge chunk of his life was missing. But it seemed, when you added it up, he must have met some people who lived the Buddha's way and brought it back with him. Or he did not like his clothes and worked it all out like the prince had. Either way, some books said all the man Jesus was talking about was being an enlightened human, like Buddha, and that we can either make life heaven or hell.

It seemed my mother had made her life quite hellish, for sure. Maybe Him is a buddhist, I thought. Maybe I will ask Him when I see him. The clothes put on me were far from the thoughts that this way of life taught. Because of my religion, my tribe spoke badly of others and thought they were better, and others spoke badly and hated us. Because of my family background and class, others, who were lower than us, were less than us, and they hated us. The constant bad words that came from the adults about others behind their backs were just as bad as if anyone did the same to them, of which they constantly complained about. How could people stop hating others, if that was all they did? I swore to myself that I would never be like this when I grew up. My family would watch the news and speak with such hate for an Arab country when it had done nothing to them.

"They should just bomb the lot of them," they would say.

But what about the children? The mothers and grandpas? I thought. Were they to be killed for a hate of something that seems to have never hurt me. It seems the clothing of hate is passed down from parent to child and continues without any actual real reason. This always hurt me to hear my parents talk badly of others who had not done anything to them. It made me see how it would never actually stop anything bad because the hate made others hate. Living in the past hate made the future more of the same. If everyone stopped hating, then the hate would stop.

This would make me feel much stronger about getting to a point in my life when I could take off the clothing of hate and be my own person, my real truth. I saw anger in the faces of people who spoke about others and wondered why would anyone want to carry that? It was like a weight of ugliness. I had non-Jewish friends and black friends and poor friends, and it made me feel ashamed of my clothes. Did speaking bad in private make them feel better? Why did they need to feel better? Were they not good enough inside? What good did bad and hate do? It all seemed to make no sense. We were all born the same. Babies with no clothes. But, sometimes, I even found myself joining in the bad jokes, just to fit in and not be laughed at for not doing so. A lie of putting down others to fit in with others. The pressure to fit in and be liked was too much. I was in a prison of what other people thought about me. I could not be who I really was. I had to be a part of the crowd or be laughed at as crazy. It was a trick to keep me stuck in the middle. Frightened to be true to me. Frightened to see the sense in the non-sense. Frightened to stand up and stop the hate wars. I could not be a Buddha, like the prince, with all this clothing on.

CHAPTER SIX

I came in from school and put my bag down. I called for Sunny, but he didn't come. I ran into the back room, and he was in his bed. His tail began to wag, but I knew he was not well. I lay down beside him and cuddled as close as I could. He smiled, and Sunny did, also. I felt it. He was with me again. I stroked Sunny and noticed the lump on his side had gotten bigger. My mother walked in from the kitchen with a sad face. She waited for me to come home, so we could take him to the vet together. As soon as Sunny knew we going to get in the car he jumped up as if nothing was wrong. Maybe it's not so bad. Maybe he's just tired, I thought.

"Everything changes, and nature has it's seasons," Him said as we rode in the car.

I looked to my mum who, of course, had not heard any of this.

"We are part of nature, and all animals also. It's just the way the world is created. The way it is all designed. But as you know, from knowing me, it is not all as it seems or all that is seen. There is light we can't see and sounds we can't hear and other senses we don't use. You don't see me or hear me but know and experience all that I am."

As I rode in the car hugging Sunny, while he had his head out the window loving the breeze, I listened with every tiny part of my body to Him. I was becoming aware of another world within our world and noticing that our world might just be, well, like a dream. A dream that most have no idea about. Maybe He was helping me wake from the dream. Maybe we wake up when we die. That would be a nice surprise.

When we got to the vet and my mum opened the door, Sunny jumped out of the car, and his tail wagged. Inside, after enjoying and stroking all the other dogs and cats other people had brought in, it was our turn to go in to see the vet. Mr. Todd, the vet, was always the nicest grown-up I knew. He was always funny and always loved Sunny. And Sunny loved him, too. He wagged his tail and gave him a nice lick as he bent down to say hello. He ran his hands along where the lump was and agreed that it had gotten bigger. There was some talk of some medicine, but he also said it could be very hard on them. If he was eating and still happy, then that was a good sign, he said. Mum decided against the harsh treatments, and Mr. Todd agreed. As long as Sunny was happy, it was just the way it was. My mother asked, or tried to, without me understanding, but the answer the vet gave was obvious to me. I understood because I knew Him was there at the very moment, and everything was as it was, and it really was all wonderful, right there and then. Unless, I let my mind take me to a frightened, sad place. I was very calm. I suppose being mad and upset was just not being able to do anything about something bad. In the car, I decided to tell Mum that everything was going to be wonderful and that Sunny and I knew. She looked at me, and then at Sunny with a smile and a tear in her eyes. I just hugged Sunny, and Him joined in for the love of it all.

CHAPTER SEVEN

I was reading more and more about the prince who walked away from his riches and found peace. His way of life made a lot of sense when I watched how most people lived with so much stress in all their clothing. Everyone was busy trying to be something they were not. My mind was getting calmer than it used to be. Quieter. My brothers beating on me would always fade away, and my mother rarely had to hit me with the spoon anymore, because I was not so bad. I knew, in time, I could free myself from the clothing of others and dress myself, and live how I wanted. I knew that all the words given to me from others, were words passed down by others to them. The brainwashing of layers of the game of clothes.

"It's your duty; it's tradition. What would your grandfather say? How are you going to support a family? Life's not easy. Money doesn't grow on trees. Do you know how much it costs to send you to this school?"

If I knew I would have had all this put on me, I might never have wanted to be born. But I had no choice. It seemed there was this invisible book of rules, of fenced-in mind games that everyone sticks to and so everyone thinks it's normal. Always having to keep others happy. To do what others want for you. To be what they think is right for you. To have no choice in your own choices.

Anyway, one afternoon, I was playing with my soldiers in my room. Mum did not allow us to watch much TV, which I am glad of. My imagination was always in use, and I was always being creative.

I was just in the middle of running over a toy, sniper, soldier with a toy tank, when Him came to me. I can imagine the prince who left his riches might've found Him. Maybe he did? When Him is around, it was like a peaceful calm. The clothes fell off.

"Your imagination will be your future. Your creativity will be your life. And you will find what you know you want through that."

I looked around, as I always did, just, maybe, in the hope, Him would show himself. But Him never did. He was there but not in our normal world. Not in the world of ears, nose, and eyes or even touch. His world was far more smarter than these simple human ways.

"The prince and I met. Numerous names from the past have been allowed to experience me, and many more without knowing. They write, paint, sing, and create amazing things that humans have enjoyed over thousands of years. "

He answered all my questions before I could ask.

"The clothes are all part of the lie of it all. The game. Imagine taking them off, without fear, or guilt or worry. This is like the caterpillar turning into the butterfly. It can happen in life but rarely does. But it will always happen in the end, as you call it. But there is no actual end."

He smiled a big, smile. I laughed, and Him was gone. I think I had an idea now. I was a caterpillar. Held down, sluggish, and frightened. But slowly, with courage, I could find what the prince found. This is a journey of either staying clothed or taking them off and being freer, lighter. That weightless feeling would be the butterfly. It was like the jigsaw puzzle of it all was being put together, piece by piece. To try and explain this to anyone would be quite difficult. Maybe it's up to each of us to find out for ourselves? But why me? Why not my mum or my Dad? They were much older and still angry and stressed at everything. Maybe, one day, I will write a book, so others can know. Well, not know, but know someone else who knows. And maybe it might help them to remember. Like I read the book of the story of the prince, others could read my story. As my mind drifted into my future, my mother's angry shout echoed through the house to come down for dinner. It was always okay for her to shout up to us. But when I would shout down for something, she would always say, "Don't shout. Come down stairs if you want to speak to me."

The silliness of it all. My brother said it was called hippo crazy or something. Some time in the future, she put in an intercom system all over the house. The same thing happened. If I did not use it, she shouted for me to do so. But, when she shouted from downstairs up to me, I dared not tell her to use the intercom. Very hippo crazy. Anyway, I left my toy battlefield and fell back into the bad fitting clothes of it all. Thoughts took over again. Useless thoughts. Fearful thoughts. Why does my mind do this? Why can't it stay awake and clear? As I left my room to get to the stairs, I was suddenly ambushed with a dead arm punch from my oldest, not so smarter brother. I nearly did what I had always done in the past, but I found myself in a moment of frozen slow motion clearness. Time stood still, and I did not react. I just stopped, held my arm, smiled, and said, "I forgive you."

My brother's evil smile dropped. I walked down the stairs and watched him stand like a confused animal.

"Come on. Dinner is ready," I said. And he walked behind me, down the stairs. As we sat down he seemed to be a little lost. It's like he did not need to bully anymore. It became useless to him. He ruffled my hair and said, "You're funny, you are."

I smiled.

That must be a good thing, to be funny. That was a good meal. Mum seemed to be soft, and my brothers all enjoyed that fact as much as me. Maybe, when she was not happy, my brothers took that on, and because they became unhappy they used it to make me unhappy. Imagine if the whole world was happy, how wonderful it would always be for everyone. If only I could make mum always happy, then we could all be happy. If only Him would meet Mum and let her know. I would be willing to not ever meet Him again if he would do that, I thought. Then, Him smiled. I felt it. I smiled. My bother looked at me and saw me smile. My mother saw my brother look at me and she looked at me.

"What are you looking so happy about? Did you just find the secret to life in your eggs and chips?" she said.

My brother ruffled my hair again.

"He's gone all funny today," he said.

I smiled as I dunked my chip into the egg and the yellow ran all over the plate.

"It's all going to be wonderful," I said.

My mum laughed a laugh so loud and fantastic that my brothers seem to catch it like an instant cold. It was true. Mum being happy was where we become happy. That meal was one of those meals I will never forget. Both my brothers started to laugh at Mum laughing, and no one knew why we were laughing and so we laughed at that. My mum had tears rolling down her face and my older brother found it so funny he fell backwards off his chair, which made my other brother spit out his drink and it just got louder and more and more giggly. Through my tears and pain from my tummy hurting so much, I looked at my mum and saw her giggling like a little girl. She was so wonderfully, beautiful when she was happy. Sunny was now standing by the table, and his tail was wagging like crazy, and his smile was bigger than ever. Even Him smiled more than ever. Everything was wonderful, for those few minutes. I wondered if this is what normal families do all the time? How nice it would be, to be free of all the silliness and just be silly. In the end, Mum had to go into the kitchen as she was in so much pain from laughing. Finally we ran out of laughter, but it seemed we were drunk with smiles. Happiness was catching. My calm infected my brothers and my mother. This was the Prince's way. I did not react to my brother after the ambush, so we did not come to the table fighting, which did not make mum scream. Life changed direction from simply changing my reaction. Wow. I think I just had a moment that the prince must have had. Nothing but me could bring happiness but me. I could create misery by reacting or happiness by not reacting. Well, I did react but not badly. I took the fight out of it. It was a Buddha reaction, maybe. It was just a punch. It was like all the others. It was the same pain, but different reaction. I changed my mind. I managed to stop me from being the normal me and become a new me. It seems the reaction is what brings the problems. I did not add to the problem. I stopped me wanting to call him a name back. If I could make sure I could be able to not react, I could make a life with more calm and happiness.

CHAPTER EIGHT

To be able to watch my reactions was all I needed to do. But of course the weight of the clothes and everyone else's reactions around me would be so loud that I would get lost in the noise of it all. I think this was the wonderful Him was talking about. I tried my hardest to watch my mind. I think we have two of them. The prince saw this. One, is the one that is full of the clothes of others, and most just wear them, no matter how ill fitting, and the other mind is the one that knows it's all a lie, all un true. The mission would be hard, because I would keep falling backwards, like a bad habit. Being enlightened was what the books in the library kept saying. Maybe everyone is in the dark before they can become it? Maybe the other mind, the one that watched, was the light that needed to end the dark? It's very difficult to change life, when living life surrounded by people who are all in the dark. It was all one huge bad habit, of bad habits mixed together to confuse and keep the light out.

One day, I asked if I could go out on my skateboard. No one wore helmets in those days. Anyway, my last memory was waving goodbye to my mum at the door. After that, the only thing that I remembered (before I rang the door bell on my return and I saw my mum's face of horror), was the memory of being with Him. I was not with me, of me, on the ground, or anything I could describe, but I was fine and wonderful. Then, after seeing my mother's shocked face at the front door when I came back, the next thing I remember was being wheeled through a hospital in a wheel chair and with a golf ball size lump on the front of my head. I never remembered what happened. But I did know it would all be wonderful. There was a comfort now surrounding everything. Sometimes I would fall into the dark mind and in an instant a candle would be lit and a smile would brighten my mind and the worry thoughts would vanish. I heard a song in the car on the way back from the hospital, which my mother was singing along to. It was a very simple song. But the three words of the title that were sang all the way through it made me know that Him had something to do with the creation of the song. That Him had, somehow, met the singer. Even when my mother sang it, she lit up with joy and tears of happiness oozed out of her eyes down her face. It was a message to all of us about all of life. It was the simple truth of the lie of our bad reactions. This was quite amazing.

"This is telling us not to worry, stress, hate or anger," I said to my mum.

"I Know," she said.

"If only it could be so easy," she said.

This song became my tune, my special message to me to bring myself out of the darkness in my mind. All I would do would be to sing it, as it's sung, again and again. "Let it be, let it be, let it be, let it be...simple words of wisdom. My own secret, to help me change my mind and not mind. It seems everything we do that brings pain in the mind is not letting it be. So, this was a new practice to change the bad habit into a good habit.

When we got home, as the door opened, I expected Sunny would be right there to welcome me from my visit to the hospital, but it seemed we had to turn right around and rush him to the vet.

I went into the back room where he was, in his bed. His tail was just about wagging and his eyes were too sad to even look at. I cried in an instant and screamed for my mum to help. She had to pick him up and I helped. In the car, I wanted Him to come to me to help me feel okay. I tried singing the song, but I couldn't let it be. I just wanted Sunny to be Sunny. Mum wanted me to stay at home and rest, but I refused. She was shouting about the world.

"First the boy. Now the dog. What did I do to deserve this? "

On top of my terrible headache, the fuzziness of the pills they gave me, and Sunny being sick, Mum was now making me feel bad. I didn't mean to hurt myself. I hugged Sunny and wished I could click my heals three times like in the Wizard of Oz and be somewhere else. Somewhere that was homely and warm and did not have angry words. Sunny was hugging me back with love and this was my home. To me, Sunny was my heaven. No war could harm me if I was hugging him.

Mum double parked the car, jumped out and screamed at the person in the car behind in such a way that I don't think if they were even eight feet tall they would get out of the car. She opened the back door, and we both carried Sunny inside. They were very helpful, and everyone who was waiting allowed us to go straight in front of them. My mother did say sorry to them, very nicely. It was all too much for me. I needed to sit down, as I felt dizzy. Right there and then, in the vet backroom, I just sat down on the floor and closed my eyes. I wished Him would come. I wished Him would help me. Mum was now very upset about me as the vet looked at Sunny. I opened my eyes and told her I was fine, just tired, and very sad. She kissed my head and told me not to stand up too quickly. She explained to the vet about our visit to the hospital, and he was even nicer and kinder than ever. I did not want anything to happen to Sunny. Not yet. I was not ready. I had no one, or nowhere to go without him. I was drowning in fear.

A few injections later and Sunny seemed to find his smile again. They were going to keep him overnight and do some tests. I asked to stay with him, but that was not allowed, and I had to get some rest myself, so I was told. On the way back in the car, HE came to me.

"It's not for you, for him to stay. It's just a time to move on. Don't see it as a bad thing. You will take his goodness and his love and find strength in his not being there for you. Just when the caterpillar thought it was over."

I looked at Mum as she drove, and she had no idea. I turned back and thought about what he said. I think, I was being selfish. Sunny had no control over this.

"It's all going to be wonderful!" Him said again. I smiled.

"What are you smiling about? " Mum asked.

"It's all going to be wonderful!" I said.

I think my mother thought I was still a little damaged. She shook her head.

"I think someone needs a good long night's sleep and some medicine."

We smiled at each other. Him smiled also.

"Nothing is what you think it is. It's all an illusion. Like a magic trick. A lie, a dream, even. If I am real to you, yet no one hears, feels, or sees me, are you dreaming it all, or is it real? From an ant to the dolphins in the sea. From the crow in the sky to Sunny. All creatures live in a place without the crowded thoughts that humans do. They don't require a clock and don't hold onto the past or worry of the future. They are free in the moment that never ends. If a human could find this place, they would find the place that the prince found. Letting it be, lets it be. Some smart human once wrote, 'To be or not to be?' Being is where life is lived. Wishing, hoping, wanting, needing, worrying, angering and hating are all being somewhere else."

The sun was going down, and it started to rain just as we drove into the driveway.

"If you imagine that inside your mind is stuck with thoughts, why not let them slide away, unstuck? They are only thoughts. What is a thought? Is it real, like Sunny, or is it just a dream inside your head?"

And then, Him was gone. I listened and watched inside my mind. I was being very much like Him said and not thinking of anything or being anywhere, but where I was, in the moment of that moment. My shoulders stopped hunching and my sadness and worry seemed to slide off into the nowhere inside my head. It all became very clear. Like a fog had lifted. I opened the car and looked at my mum's face that was wrinkled and worried with worry. It was like she was carrying a weight of nothing. A heavy weight of thoughts. But these sticky worries seemed to be aging her. As we walked into the house the rain and its sound became all there was for a few moments, then my mind started to think about how all animals are in the moment of now and maybe Sunny is, and also he must be letting it be, so is not really thinking sad or worried thoughts. This is the prince's way.

"Get upstairs and run a bath. I will heat you some chicken soup," my mother said softly.

The magical soup was an incredible power in a bowl. Maybe it was the many years of grandma saying it was magic, and maybe her grandma before her, as well as Mum saying it was magic, that had us all believing it was magic, and so it actually was. Like a hypnosis through the ages. Once I drank from the bowl, I was always much better. Colds and sickness would just go away. Why did we need doctors? The phone started to ring, and my mother screamed very quickly at me not to answer it. I don't think she was in the mood for anything else today. As I got to the top of the stairs, my older brother came out. He spoke to me like he had not done for a very long time. Like he was actually my real brother and not the bully who thought he was better than me. I suppose being hurt and being sad brings another side out of other people. Maybe this is his real side and the other is an act. Like another set of clothes on top of the clothes. He scruffed up my hair and offered his room to me. Now, this was like a ticket to Disney land for me. Although I had a headache and was tired and also sad for Sunny and missed him, I was feeling calm. There really was no actual problem there and then, in that moment. In fact, it was a moment of better than normal because I saw it that way, as well as my brother being so nice. The other side, to the two sides of life. The full picture not drowned out by thoughts. This was a new way to see. A new eye, or ear, in a way. I looked up and thanked Him. He smiled. I was aware of me being me, and so I could make a choice to be a happier me. Why choose not to be? Under the bad stuff, the dark stuff, there was always the light. It was just waiting there. Why did we like to be in the dark so much? Maybe it was just practiced into. A bad habit of not seeing the other us. The prince had to walk away and find his new habits. Maybe we think it's natural to be in the dark because we don't know the light? Because we grow up being showed everything by those who don't know. So, it just keeps happening, again and again. He smiled.

    I did not have to go to school for a week. Sunny came back the next day and seemed to be as good as new. He was on a new medicine. I knew somehow that it was not forever, but I also knew it was meant to be this way. Sunny and I spent virtually every moment of the week together. It was like the chicken soup. He watched me play Lego and my stuffed monkey Charlie and him battled pretend battles. We watched some TV, but not much, as Mum said it would make us stupid.

"Children should be outside. Rain or shine," she would say.

So Sunny and I dug in the mud, in the garden, and he watched me turn over big rocks and see the other world of ants, spiders, and crawly things. I wondered about what Him said about all creatures. I watched them moving around. They have no clothes. Does an ant have to be anything else on top of being an ant? Is a spider told what he must and must not do or who to pray to? Do the wood lice speak badly of the other crawling creatures? They all seemed to get on, under this rock. No anger or hate. They must think? They must know? They must have some feelings. I lowered the rock slowly and my mind came back to the other world. As it did, Him was there.

"The other world, as you seem to think, is the same. There is no divide. Like you have made borders on this planet, you do so in your mind of other creatures and other humans. There was a time when you did not separate the land. Many Indians and people living off nature still feel the land does not belong to them, but they are part of it. The land, the sea, and the air are all one. All exist connected to each other and living off each other so that they can be. This is for the earth and the moon and the earth to the sun. The connection continues and never ends. Everything is one thing and everything is everything in itself. Your head requires your heart, and your hands require your mind, and your mind requires you. But you are also more than your body and mind, as you know by meeting me. Humans labeled themselves human beings, but they are trying, wanting, needing to be something else, always. To be or not to be? Remember?" Him smiled. I smiled. Sunny smiled.

Everything was everything, and I was also part of it all. My body seemed to vanish into the blur of it all, and I felt like no time or space really existed. My mind made them up. Everyone's mind did. So if everyone's mind can make everything seem broken and in bits and not part of the same thing, maybe if everyone found the light, it would all fix itself. It's quite confusing but quite simple. A magic trick of knowing hidden in every person.

I went inside and Sunny followed. My brothers were sitting at the table, looking like frightened sheep, and my mother was on the phone not looking happy. More trouble from the courts and solicitors. The phone was slammed down, and I was screamed at to sit down for tea. Some toast and orange drink. Even Sunny knew things were not worth sticking around for, so he was lucky enough to leave the room and find a bunker somewhere else. He left at the right time. The air was very thick and heavy. I'm not sure what actually created the explosion, but it seemed to happen out of nowhere. Just as I was spreading my chocolate spread on my toast, Mum screamed and threw a whole cup of tea, with cup up to the ceiling. It smashed and went everywhere. She then stormed out of the room leaving us three in shock. My brother leaned over and took the chocolate spread jar, and we continued for a moment in silence. But out of this came another one of those moments when we became joined in our bunker of the war. Our eyes kept looking at each other. The tea dripped from the ceiling above us and had stained a big brown blob. My older brother let out a giggle that he very quickly covered with his hand. That was it. Fear and shock turned into inside giggles. I had to leave the table and started to clean up the broken cup all over the room in the hope I might stop laughing. My other brothers both went in different directions to also escape. One upstairs, and one out into the garden. It was funny for us, as well as sad. That tea stain remained on the ceiling for quite a while. In fact, once, another time, we were sat eating ice lollies, and my brother spoke and pointed with his lolly in his hand, and it slipped right off the stick into the air and landed right in the middle of the tea stain, and got stuck. This time, Mum laughed with us. A stain, on a stain, on the ceiling. Not long after that, the ceiling was repainted.

CHAPTER NINE

Dad had moved to a new house, and it was quite far away from where he lived before. This caused more problems because he said a lot of his time was spent driving to pick us up and bring us back and he needed more time. But Mum said he should have thought about that before he bought the house. My dad then said that, if he did not have to pay so much to her, he could afford to live closer. Mum did not answer, but smiled. The war of words shot backwards and forwards without any care for us in the middle. It was like everything was our fault. We were the ammunition. They were both trying to make their point and both trying to be better and win. There never seemed to be a winner because they were always angry afterwards. To me, I shrank inside. And wished I could continue to shrink into nothing. I just wanted peace. I didn't ask for this, but I had no choice. It was like the air was always ten times heavier. I promised myself every time there was an explosion, I would never put my children through this if I ever even have a family. Do parents have any idea what nasty words being screamed feel like to a little boy? Always anger and hate. Bitter sounding words and nastiness. It was making my mind muddled up. Was this how all love ended? At least, I had Sunny. He was my protection. One hug with him and all the pain vanished and I was lost in the everything of it all. The everything that Him told me about. It's always there under the noise. Like the sun is always there on a cloudy day. Somewhere, hidden.

Sunny was starting to get tired quickly and we could not go out for long walks. Even his face seemed to be older all of a sudden. Sometimes, I would just bury my head in his chest, and hug and cry into him. And Him was always there. It always started as sad and always seemed to turn into a crying with happiness. He managed to make it all seem okay. I knew it was. I knew it would be, but part of me wanted to have Sunny forever. Who would I go to? How could I survive the war? There was a lesson to all of this as Him had said, but I did not want to learn right now. I wanted Sunny to be here for me, always. Then, he spoke.

"The one thing about life most don't understand is they don't see it right. The clothes, and the fear that they bring, take them away from the connection to it all. To the all and everything that they are part of. They are lost. Again, am I real or imaginary? If I'm real then there is more to this life than what you imagine. This imaginary life you lead, leads you to somewhere, and it is never the final that you think. If you are asleep, a dream is real. While you are awake, life feels real. Both are real, but it's our state in our mind that changes. We are still us. One is a waking dream the other a dreaming dream. But both are as real as the other. The truth, as you see it, is the love of Sunny, not the thing of him. It's a feeling that we all have, always, inside, all the time. Yet we look to things to bring it to the surface. We have lost the connection to it and so need switches to give us quick feelings of it."

I kind of understood. My mind seemed to expand inside like a balloon every time Him came to me. I was sure this was how the prince found his way. I looked at Sunny and he looked at me with his tired face. He smiled and we all smiled, and it was the answer to everything in an instant.

"It's all going to be wonderful," Him said. And then he was not there.

I looked at Sunny.

"I think I have to somehow stay in the mind I am in, when Him is around, when he is not around. Then I won't fall asleep and be in the wrong mind. Then life won't hurt so much," I said to Sunny.

If only I could help Mum with her life. She was tired with all the bad feelings. All the people like my mum who stressed all the time looked more wrinkled. Is this the weight of life? I don't want to carry all that with me. We had an uncle who lived in Spain, and, when he came to London, he always looked happy and healthy. I think the sunshine must help. Also living by the sea. For some reason, stress was not worn on the faces of people who seemed happy.

Dad's new home was on the other side of London. Over the river Thames. Near where they played tennis every year. A place called Wimbledon. It was nice. Lots of green everywhere. A nice town, and not so much traffic. He had three floors in the house. But it was skinnier than a normal two floor one. We were given sweets and chocolate, and he had the biggest collection of videos. It was like Aladdin's cave. Free to enjoy the treasures of it all. I think he was buying our love by letting us do and have everything Mum wouldn't, but I didn't say anything. I think my brothers would hit me, for sure. We sat down to watch James Bond, Gold Finger, for the hundredth time, but we all loved it. My Dad thought he was a Sean Connery look-a- like and pretended he was Bond. Always puffing up his chest and seeming to be big and saying the words from the TV in a very bad Scottish accent. Eventually, in time, he did so well in his business that he went and bought an Aston Martin car. Now he was always puffed up, and it was like he wanted everyone to see him for what he had. Like his car was him and made him special or better. He would always give people big tips and so always got treated well wherever we went. It seems he was buying the love of everyone else, not just us. Mum was never flash, and this was very obvious. I did enjoy the lie of it all, when with Dad, but also thought it was wrong to think that having some money and wearing expensive clothes and driving a flash car would make you feel better than others. And funnily enough it made others treat my Dad like a king. Like they actually felt less than him. People thinking they are bigger and better by what religion they are, what color they are, what they own, what they do, what they wear. It was crazy. It made everyone break up and join groups and fight and talk badly of each other. Grandparents hated, so parents hated, and then the kids joined in the hate. Everyone talked about wanting world peace, but how can we have peace if we are in pieces? I made a pact with myself that when I grew up and became someone special, I would share all I could with everyone else. Spread it around and make it more even. But the feeling that came over me when we got new expensive clothes or sat in the car was the funny thing. It was very clear that I was in a pretend act. Look at me, I'm better, I'm bigger. It's like I could not stop me wanting to feel more. It was another me. A me who loved to be more. Maybe, I did not think enough of me in the first place? Then I thought about it. At home I could make myself bigger by doing things to get mum to think of me as good. Which made my brothers seem less good. At school if you were better at one thing you got to be in a better class and they looked down and teased those who were not so good.

Everyone was in a race to be better and more. Was this the rat race? And because of the race everyone was busy not being them self or not being truthfully happy, but trying too hard to be something more. And, because there was always others with more it was never ending. Maybe it should be called the hamster wheel race? We knew rich people and they always complained about everyone and everything. It's like, once you get so high up, no one is good enough and nothing is done right. I would rather be happy than have all that complaining and moaning.

Anyway. Bond was always great, and I liked the ladies and the silly names they had. He was my hero, I suppose. Maybe one day I could be on the TV and play James Bond, or someone like him, I thought. We had some smoked salmon and cream cheese bagels and some Coca-Cola,(which mum did not allow us to have in the house), so I drank as much as I could. In the car, on the way back, I sat in the back with one of my brothers as my oldest brother sat upfront. Every now and then, he would lean back and punch my leg and my other brother would do it straight after. All my dad would say was "take it like a man. Be tough.' Dad was always making me punch his hand, telling me not to cry, and saying, be a man. And Mum was always saying it's good to cry and not be ashamed. I wanted to be tough, but I did not want to not feel what I felt about happy or sad things. Then I felt Him around me just for a second, and I smiled. It just made me stop thinking confusing bad thoughts. Thoughts that went nowhere but make me stress in my mind. When He smiled, I saw my thoughts for their silliness and my mind got unstuck.

We got to a lot of traffic at Battersea Bridge, which my Dad did not like, but I got to sit up and see the River Thames in both directions. It was always amazing. And I heard that it's impossible to swim from one side to the other because the currents were very strong. I was a good swimmer. We all were. Mum made sure of that after she nearly drowned as a child. I swam for the school and the Cub Scouts, before I got told to leave. I liked my swimming but not the training. I also liked my Judo and did competitions around the country. I did gymnastics for a few years and also traveled around the country doing competitions, but it all stopped when I had to get serious about my school work.

As we pulled up to our house the anticipation of Dad pulling out a large bundle of money was quite amazing. Like the lions at feeding time in the zoo. I did feel a little guilty, but knew it was my payment for the war I was being put in. I could see the curtains twitch as mum sneaked a peak at us in the car, and I could see Dad see the curtains move. This made him take his time to make sure mum got annoyed. They both played the same games with each other and we always got shouted at about it.

Eventually the front door would open. We could not see Mum, as she did not want to see Dad. He would get out the car and walk us half way down the drive. Just so he could step on her land. When we got inside the hate and bad words would start. And this time, unlike any other, I had a special cloak of invisibility. I remembered to stay awake, to not fall asleep. To know it would all be wonderful.

"It's a passing cloud in the sunny day called life," He said.

I smiled as everything slowed down and my mother's screams became more muffled and quiet to me. It really was like I could control how I reacted to others reacting badly. Then, just like with the time when I did not go mad at my brother for punching me, my mother stopped.

She looked at me. I smiled at her.

"It's all going to be wonderful," I said.

She smiled and we had the biggest strongest hug. She even started to laugh.

This was now the test. Always be awake. Never fall into the other mind, which makes others become angry, bad or unhappy. This, the Buddhist called a practice. Then, just as I was stopping hugging my mum, He spoke again.

"Bee the honey, not the sting." he said.

Then the most incredible thing happened. My mother spoke.

"I like that. Very good. Who told you that? Bee the honey not the sting," she said.

She heard Him!

"I didn't say anything. It was Him. I wanted to tell you about Him," I said excitedly.

But the look on my mum's face told me she had no idea what I was talking about, and I quickly decided to let it be, and not ruin the wonder of it all. She heard. Wow. Maybe it was the hug. I looked up and all around me. I smiled. He smiled, everything smiled. And everything was wonderful. And not only was it wonderful, it was my proof that He was real. He existed outside of my life. It was not just in my head. It was like He really, truly made me believe everything he had ever said in that one moment. Like a switch got turned on. The curtains were pulled open, and the sunlight came streaming in.

CHAPTER TEN

Life was now lighter. It was like I had space all around me. I was part of it all and kind of felt it all. It was like there was two of me. And so two worlds I could live in. I knew the silence was there behind everything and space was in between it all. There was a calm around all the normal, angry, things around me. I think my brothers thought I was mad. Mum was still always stressed, but she seemed to always be more peaceful around me now. Maybe it was rubbing off. Now and then she would say, "Bee the honey!" and smile, but I could see she was pretending. Everything was the same around me, but I was now somehow not being caught in all the traps of it all. It was like stepping outside of me. It was like I was more than just my mind and thoughts. Maybe there is a place where the mind lives, but it does not know it lives there? Maybe the clothes are the puzzle in the mind that we have to solve to get to this place.

I was sitting in the garden, and Sunny was next to me. It was a warm day and everything was alive around me. We never stop and see and feel nature. We just walk around it and ignore it. Without the sky and clouds and wind, the trees and flowers and seeds would not be able to do what they do to keep being more trees, flowers and seeds. And without these, the bees and flies and birds would not be able to be there. Everything was part of one big working wonder of being. It was like a dance of nature. A design. And of course us humans need all of it to be able to live. Yet we don't notice them, and, because of this, we are not connected like we should be. And because of this, we stop caring for them. If we looked after our nature maybe there would be less problems in life. It seems that we are just as bad to our self, as we are to the world we live in and live off.

If I allowed me to fall into my mind and then get trapped in all the thoughts, I would start to find it all became heavy again. But if I stayed awake and noticed the space and silence and knew it was all going to be wonderful, it always seemed to clear and get lighter. It was my new hobby. My new practice. Was this what the prince found? Was this why Him came to me? Whatever I had found, was always here. It was like my radio was tuned into a different place. I just needed to fine-tune it and not listen to the noise, but the space it all came from. Sunny rested his head on my leg as we sat on the grass and enjoyed the sunshine. He now seemed to be much more than a fluffy hairy dog. Whenever we were together I was in a better place. Maybe Sunny was trying to tell me all the time that it was always here. Mum called from the back door for me to come in and bring the dog for his dinner. I got up and called Sunny. But he just lay there. I called him again and again. He still had his sad eyes, but they had a smile. I tried to lift him but he was all floppy. He looked at me, and my heart cried instantly. It was like he told me. The tears came straight up out of my heart and out of my eyes. I knew. We looked at each other and for some reason I smiled. Sunny smiled. And then Him smiled.

"I know," I shouted before he could speak.

I lay down beside Sunny and hugged him with all my love and all my might. I tried to give him my life. If I could give him some of my life that I would live, then I would surely be happy with less just to keep him with me a little longer.

I knew Him was all around, but he was silent. I was going to scream at Him and beg to have more time, but something came over me. All of a sudden the pain and fear turned into love. I was crying and hugging Sunny and I was okay with it. It was like we were thanking each other for each other and it was the best gift we could give each other. It was every birthday and every Christmas morning all rolled into one. Mum came out and shouted again and came towards us. I turned around and mum went from angry to instant tears. She ran and lay down and looked at Sunny.

At the vet, Sunny was in the back room with some tubes coming out of his legs. His eyes were very sad and very red and nearly closed. The vet spoke with my mum and said that we would have to wait five minutes and see if the drugs had any effect, but if not...And he went quiet. I would wait with Sunny. I would not leave him. They both went into the vet's front room. I looked around for Him, but nothing. I wanted to be angry. I wanted a reason. I wanted Him to help me. But then I became awake from it all. I knew what was happening. Sunny had told me in the garden. He had told me. It was nothing else but love or anger, Love or fear. I was frightened to be alone and not have my safe place. I was frightened to not have my friend there whenever I needed him. I was frightened I would not know how to survive. But if I knew it was all going to be wonderful, if I truly knew it, as Him had explained, and Sunny had agreed, over and over again, all the fear seemed to vanish into love. I gave Sunny my truth in the biggest bear hug I could give. I sat back and looked at him with tears rolling down my face. And then something quite amazing and incredible happened. Sunny turned into light. He was there and a light was there, but the light just drifted out of him upwards and through the ceiling. I went numb. I was wide awake and more alive then I had ever been. The door opened from the front room and my mother and Mr. Todd walked in. The vet leaned down and checked on Sunny. He looked back at my mum and tears fell out of her eyes like a waterfall.

"I'm sorry. I'm going to have to put him to sleep," he said.

At that very moment, Sunny stopped breathing. I didn't even know I was listening but when it stopped I noticed. My mum kneeled next to me and we cried and cried. I knew it was not an end. I knew it was more than breath. I knew. And then Him was there. And not only Him, but Sunny was there. And we were all there, all wrapped in each other and it was wonderful. And it all became clear. It's all about finding the love and not letting the fear take us over. It's all about knowing there is more and that we are all part of it. It's about seeing through the mist of clothing put on us. It's about not letting the noise cover the truth. Right there, as I lay hugging Sunny, I knew he was gone, I saw him leave, but I hugged the old him because that was all I could do. But he was still with me. Still in me. Still in my heart. I cried a mixed cry of sadness and happiness. It was the most incredible feeling. And Him cried with me. He cried so wonderfully. Right there, in the worst moment of my life, I knew it was all going to be wonderful. I missed Sunny already but knew that was just silliness because he was with me, part of me, and always was and always will.

After this I seemed to be much happier. I did not tell anyone of the light that came out of Sunny because they would make fun of me. And somehow I knew that later in life it would be a great story to be able to tell. The same craziness continued around me with my family, but I kept myself awake and did not allow it to stick to me and drag me down. I felt like the prince under the tree.

Three months later, we got a new puppy. He was another golden retriever. When my mum told me that he was in the other room, for one second I felt like a traitor and felt myself getting sad and angry because of Sunny, but I did not let it stick. I laughed at not loving. When I opened the door and went into the hall this bundle of clumsy white and golden fluff came bouncing towards me. And it was quite the most wonderful thing. I cried and Mum cried. It was pure joy. And Him was there laughing with us.

"The love never dies. The truth is always there under the fear. It's being able to live in one and not the other that makes it a special life."

"It's all going to be wonderful," Him said.

I laughed and giggled and fell around with the puppy.

"It's all going to be wonderful, I promise," said my mum.

And we laughed together as the puppy jumped and fell and jumped and fell all around me.

I decided to call him Yogi, and soon we got a

great Dane puppy that we called Booboo. They loved each other so much, all the time. I could just sit and watch them and smile. He would come to me less, now, but I always knew he was always there. One day I will tell people about Him, and maybe they will be able to find what the Prince and I found.

                    THE END.
                    BUT NOT.

Made in United States
Orlando, FL
23 March 2025